First Printing, 2020

ISBN 9798577440831

Illustrations: Leandro Starorengo
Layout: Fresh Design

**For the free audio of Jake's Joyful loving kindness meditation, please visit michellearscottbooks.com**

Michelle Arscott

# JAKE'S Joyful Bubbles

Illustrated by
Leandro Stavorengo

Thank you to my husband Oscar
for his support with my dreams.

Thank you to my energetic boys Max and Luca,
who always provide light in my life
and not forgetting a thank you
to my beautiful dog Thomas.

Thank you to my parents and sister
for their continual love and ongoing
support for all of my projects.

Thanks to the book team Mohana Rajakumaur,
Michelle Fairbanks, Leandro Stavorengo,
Gemma Ombuya, Katie Johnson Kabage
and Rima Murray.

Jake was bored.
"Mum - will you play with me?" he asked.
"I will later," she whispered.
"Go and play outside for now."

"Will you play with me?"
Jake asked his neighbour.

"In a little while,"
said the neigbour.

Jake saw ants and
began to march.
He felt the cool breeze
on his skin and swirled
like the falling leaf.

He watched the lazy bee
resting on the flower
and began to buzz
like a bee.

Then he jumped
like a frog

but

he

fell.

"Mum," he cried.

Then he saw
the most beautiful,
green caterpillar, shuffling
along the ground.

A bubble began in his heart
and started getting
**bigger**.

He followed the caterpillar to a dandelion.
Jake picked it up to make a wish.

# WHAT ARE YOU
# GRATEFUL FOR?

# MINDFULNESS ACTIVITIES FOR KIDS

## LOVING KINDNESS
### AND
## GRATITUDE MEDITATIONS

There are many benefits of practising loving kindness meditations and gratitude activities with the children in your lives. A meditation practice or mindfulness breathing exercise is a great way to end the day on a positive note.

Practising these regularly, helps children to be calmer, to understand the power of their thoughts and actions. These meditations help them to see their role in sending positivity into the world. Other benefits include children being more grateful and positive towards other people, as well as themselves.

Find a quiet spot.

Take 3 deep dragon breaths.

Breathe in and out.

Breathe in and out.

Breathe in and out.

Feeling calm.

Imagine your heart beating inside of you.

Put your hand on your heart and feel it pumping.

Can you make a heart shape with your hand?
(Heart shape, a circle, a fist shape etc.)

Bring that heart shape towards you and breathe in and as you breathe out, push it away.

Bring your hands towards you, breathe in, push your heart shape away from you and breathe out, and again. Place your hands by your side.

Can you imagine your heart pumping?

Your heart is pumping love to the world and yourself. Your heart is such an important organ.

Now think about Jake's bubbles. Who likes bubbles? Imagine having a bubble container in your hand and a wand. You are going to blow a big bubble. Breathing in and gently out, start blowing that bubble. Every time you blow out, imagine the bubble getting bigger and bigger.

Think of someone you love, someone that makes you feel happy, imagine their face and their smile. Think of all the things that you love about that person. Maybe it's how they laugh or how they make you feel. Every time you have a nice thought about them, imagine that your bubble is getting even bigger.

Continue breathing in and out. Each time you blow out, that bubble is getting bigger and bigger with all your happy thoughts and feelings.

Now that the bubble is so big, it is time to let it go. With your hand gently push the bubble away and watch that huge bubble rising higher and higher into the sky.

That bubble is going to go now to the person that you were thinking about. Imagine that bubble bouncing off them gently. Imagine that person smiling as he or she feels your loving thoughts.

Now the bubble is breaking into lots of smaller bubbles.

Let's send those bubbles to other people. Maybe people that you know. When the bubble touches them, they are going to feel those loving thoughts and it will make them smile.

Now imagine that the bubbles are touching many people. All of them are now smiling.

You need to help those bubbles travel all around the world. So you are going to breathe in and do a big breath out. And again.

As you blow these bubbles around the world, everyone is touched by the bubbles and they are smiling as they feel your loving thoughts.

Put your hand on your heart.

Imagine a bubble is now touching you. Maybe it feels cool or a bit wet. Feel the corners of your mouth lifting. You are feeling so happy, and oh so calm as you spread love to everyone in the world, including yourself.

Now wiggle your feet and your toes and do a big stretch.

# LOVING KINDNESS MEDITATION SCRIPT
### Version for children aged 2-6 year olds.

Imagine a person who you really like.

When you think of them, how do you feel?

What colour is this feeling?

Now imagine blowing a bubble and filling it with this colour, and a feeling of love.

Every time you blow out, imagine that bubble getting bigger and bigger, filled with your feelings and this colour.

Breathe in and out and watch your bubble getting bigger and bigger.

The bubble is big enough now. Take a big breath and blow that bubble to the person you thought about. Imagine that person smile.

Watch them blow the bubble back to you.

Feel the love and colour washing over you.

Feel the warmth.

Breathe in and out.

# SHORT GRATITUDE AND LOVING KINDNESS ACTIVITIES

## GRATITUDE BREATH

Close your eyes and picture someone that you like
or love very much.

Can you see their face?

Can you see their smile?

Now as you breathe in, imagine that person,
and as you blow out, imagine blowing a big thank you
to them for being in your life.

Breathe in again and imagine that person and blow
them a big smile.

Breathe in again and blow them an even bigger smile.

Now they are blowing you a big smile back.

How does that feel?


## WISH BREATH

Think of a person you like or love. Imagine what
they look like? What are their eyes like? Are they tall
or short?

Breathe in and when you breathe out, send them a wish.

It might be a wish for them to be happy, or to laugh a lot,
or for them to be healthy.

Breathe in and as you breathe out send a happy wish
to yourself.

Now breathe in and send a wish to all your friends.

Printed in Great Britain
by Amazon